TARA LASKOWSKI

MODERN MANNERS

FOR YOUR INNER DEMONS

sfwp.com

Library of Congress Cataloging-in-Publication Data

Names: Laskowski, Tara, author.
Title: Modern manners for your inner demons / Tara Laskowski.
Description: Revised and expanded edition. | Sante Fe, NM : Santa Fe Writer's
    Project, 2017. | Series: SFWP literary awards
Identifiers: LCCN 2016028265 | ISBN 9781939650627 (softcover)
Subjects: | BISAC: FICTION / Humorous.
Classification: LCC PS3612.A857 A6 2017 | DDC 813/.6—dc23
LC record available at https://lccn.loc.gov/2016028265

Published by SFWP
369 Montezuma Ave. #350
Santa Fe, NM 87501
(505) 428-9045
www.sfwp.com

Find the author at www.taralaskowski.com

MODERN MANNERS

FOR YOUR INNER **DEMONS**

For Art and Dashiell, always

THE ETIQUETTE OF...

THE ETIQUETTE OF ADULTERY

VI. On Hotel Rooms

It is considered improper to answer the hotel phone when you are staying with him during his out-of-town work conferences. He may remind you of this, bleary-eyed at 6 a.m. on his way to a meeting, and you should nod, hold your tongue, and try not to start a fight because now is not the time for it.

After he leaves, get up and fish your panties from under the nightstand, pull on a tank top and partially open the blackout curtains. That will give you some light and some perspective. Smoke a cigarette or two and put the butts out in his coffee from last night. Turn up the heat, because it's cold in here and the Ramada is paying for it.

If the phone does ring, an annoying blaring sound, then pause and consider answering it. Picture the one photo you saw of her in his wallet a few months ago with her wavy dirty blond hair and smart little Tina Fey glasses. (Who still keeps pictures in their wallet anyway? See entry on iPhones.) Feel the thump thump in your chest, the heat that rises whenever you're about to do something naughty, and then answer it, your voice rising in a question. Don't be disappointed when it's just the front desk inquiring about a credit card charge, and don't be depressed when they call you "Mrs."

From Glossary of Terms

Pinkerson: A violent, disruptive act, usually the result of a fight, that goes beyond the normal reaction of anger. Origin—Peg and Marty Pinkerson, circa 1985, the neighbors across the street whose fights were so entertaining to you and your brother that you would've sold tickets if you could, fights that usually climaxed with one or the other Pinkerson opening a window and throwing out drawers full of nighties or dress shirts, or plowing a front tire through the tulips, or, just once, cocking a hunting rifle and promising to blow down the basement door if it didn't open by the count of ten. Colloquial use, native to you and your brother; e.g., "Dad pulled a Pinkerson last night when he threatened mom with her sewing scissors."

IV. On Comparisons

Never say, "Am I better in bed than your wife?" Instead, try, "God, you are so hot I could have sex with you three or four times a day."

Don't say, "Do I cook better than she does?" Try, "Once I had this boyfriend in college who loved French cooking so much I took a class in it just to be able to make him special meals all the time." (Even though you actually only bought a French cookbook and got frustrated when you wanted to make cassoulet and couldn't figure out where to buy duck fat. And even though said boyfriend really enjoyed going out more than staying in, which later you suspected was because he hated your cat.)

Always imagine the wife as the "other woman," and always imagine her wearing pleated pants and white nurse sneakers, snoring, and unable to throw a baseball properly.

Index — Songs for the Mourning After

IX. On Holidays

When children are in the picture (and even when they aren't), it is a generally accepted practice that he will not spend any holidays with you. It is considered desperate to drive past his house on Christmas Eve, and even more so to park a few houses down the street and watch his kids build a snowman in the backyard.

If you are lucky enough not to be born on a holiday or in the general vicinity of a holiday, then he might be with you on your birthday (see Appendix B: Lavish Gifts and Sexy Lingerie), but you will never be able to spend his birthday with him unless he travels a lot for his job.

None of this matters much for Memorial Day, Easter, Fourth of July, Thanksgiving, and hell, even Christmas. But on New Year's Eve, when everyone else at the party your friend dragged you to is pairing off to smooch at midnight, closely examine an imaginary stain on your designer jeans and drink your champagne quickly. Toss back your hair and tell yourself next year will be different.

Properly Setting the Table

Men and women should always be seated alternately around the table, unless you are having dinner with your parents, in which case it would be best to sit him next to your father, not your mother, who would start staring at the mole on the side of his neck and asking leading questions.

Prep him beforehand with easy conversation topics such as the weather, the N.Y. Giants, late-night television, how often one should get a car wash, why your father should've taken that job in Toledo when he had the chance, why your mother is glad he didn't because it meant they had you, and the shame the mayor should have on himself for the condition of the roads these days. Avoid talking about religion, the Pinkersons, and the way that your father flinches when his back twists a certain way.

Use the outside knife and fork for the appetizer, and then simply work inwards for each subsequent course. The golden rule is Always Work from the Outside In. Remember this when your mother compliments you on your sweater, because when he gets up to use the bathroom she will tell you it looks like you are getting wrinkles around your eyes and what face cream are you using these days and for crying out loud are you really still biting your nails like that.

The only proper way to cut and eat one's food is to hold the knife and fork in a relaxed, natural manner—never with clenched fists spearing food like a hunter!

Wait until all the plates and glasses have been cleared before attempting to make a getaway. Press your hand in his under the table and feel the cool smoothness of his skin, the slight indentation in his fourth finger where the ring usually sits so tightly. Hear the whish of wind threatening the thin walls, and think about Weekend In Bermuda. As he makes a sweeping comment about what a nice house they have here, see only the scarred, peeling walls marked from years of nails and thumb tacks, the unreliable generator downstairs, the worn fabric in the middle of the recliner where your father parks it every night. It's just what happens when something stays somewhere too long.

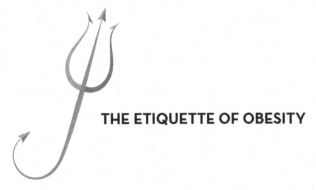

THE ETIQUETTE OF OBESITY

Preface — Origins and Anniversaries

Remember you were put on this Great Green Earth for a reason, your father said, and the animals were put on this Great Green Earth for your nourishment and for nothing else.

Hunting is not a game, he used to tell you, handing you a rifle almost as big as you. It is Serious Business. Never point a rifle at any animal unless you intend to shoot. Sit in the woods, the cold, cold woods, for hours, in silence, waiting. This is bonding time, he would say.

Accept this is not for you, even if your father never does.

Later, after he is gone, each year on opening day of deer season, take the day off work. Hole up in your bedroom with your Xbox 360 and a big bag of beef jerky. Drink Budweiser from the can and each time you open one toast to your father.

Appendix III: The Natural Habitats of Predators

1. Crowded buses

Fear of suffocation plus motion sickness plus the oppressive heat equals disaster for this quick public transportation option. Walk if you can (See Chapter 20: Exercise!) or just drive and spend the extra few dollars at the parking meter when you need to see your doctor.

2. School playgrounds

Remember the Golden Rule: Children are mean. Avoid walking by this dangerous area. Taunts such as "Chubby Checker," "Hey Fat Man," "Lard Ass," while not generally acceptable around adults, become a free-for-all when these horrible disease sacs herd in groups and are not under constant supervision.

3. Your mother's house

Hostile territory, especially around holidays when she's been "slaving away for days for you people and no one appreciates any of it." Slabs of juicy turkey, butter-laden cookies and greasy fried chicken make this a particularly perilous journey.

4. Airplanes

Get an aisle seat if you must go to Florida to see Uncle Ernie, who might pass any day now, but even then you feel boxed up, squeezed in, and your bad knee starts to throb just an hour into the flight. Remember it's not polite to lift the armrest between you and a stranger. Even so, the woman sitting beside you will most likely shift over toward the window, unwilling to touch, her eyes darting away like those deer your father tried to shoot. It's always so automatic in people, like a sea parting, everyone always so quick to step aside, shift away, outwards, leaving, departing, spiraling.

On Going Out to Eat

Never point a knife or fork at a piece of meat unless you intend to use it.

It is best to plan ahead. You can say, "I will order a salad." But then you may get there and find the salads have mushrooms on them. Then you will want a cheese steak with grilled onions and peppers and those amazing steak fries the restaurant has. Order it, but swear to yourself you will stop at half, you will only eat just a few of those fries.

It's ok, you'll work out tomorrow.

At the buffet, it is polite to yield to other hunters. If you see that another hunter already has a specific piece of meat in his sights, let him have it. Respect your peers.

Understand that not everyone hunts, and some people find the idea disgusting. You should not stop hunting, but you should exercise discretion when handling and transporting the carcass of a kill. Wrap in a napkin, push to the side of your plate. Don't pick your teeth.

XX. Exercise

Let's be frank: exercise sucks. Forget running a mile or doing push-ups when you get winded climbing the three flights of stairs to your apartment.

DO sweat the small stuff—walk uphill to the mailbox, vacuum your place each week, park in the farthest spot at the grocery store next to all the shopping carts. Do not complain about the heat in your office during the winter—sweating loses water weight!

Perhaps the best form of exercise is walking a dog. Owning a pet is one of the most satisfying decisions you will ever make, despite what your father always said about how animals should not be allowed in the house. (See Index, footnote #32).

On Dating

Try online sites like Match.com. Create a profile as honest and true to yourself as possible—mention things like your love of books and plays, your bachelor's degree in communications, the one time you went horseback riding (even though you hated it). Post a current photo, not one from seven years ago that makes you look kind of buff. It is important to Put Your Best Foot Forward, but not be deceptive.

Analyze your best assets and Get Out Into the World. Try community theater. Some roles: lead chorus, juggler number 4, barbershop owner. There are plenty of people that make it—celebrities like Danny DiVito, Dom Delouise, John Candy, that girl from the *Precious* movie that everyone loved. As your father used to say, America is the Land of Opportunity—dreams can happen.

Footnote #32

On Dog Parks — Off-leash dog parks are wonderful places for your pet to explore and play. At first your dog might hover along the edges, nervous, watchful, shy. But if after a few weeks he starts to gain confidence, smile cautiously at the woman with the black lumbering dog that your dog takes a liking to. Say, "Is it ok if they play together?" and when she nods, let your dog off the leash even though it makes you nervous.

When your legs tire of standing, sit on the park bench but do not let your dog out of your sight. Unwrap the package of powdered donuts you brought—five tiny perfect white powdered circles of fried dough. Eat them one by one, slowly, enjoying every moment of flavor bursts.

The lady with the black dog may come over. Do not hog the park bench! You will expect her to sit on the other edge as far away from you as possible, so try not to be surprised when she sits down right next to you.

For opening conversation starters, try these: "Lovely weather we've been having" or "Aren't those flowers pretty?" or "What kind of dog do you have?" Do not stare directly into her eyes, no matter how blue and mesmerizing you may find them, but don't avoid eye contact either—it makes you look shifty. Remember that time you went horseback riding—how scared you were up so high, how out of control you felt—remember it now, and take a deep breath. Offer her one of your donuts if you still have some left, and when she looks at you, really looks at you for the first time, breathe out, your chest expanding, and watch in amazement as she leans in, not out, as she brushes a bit of white powder from your lips and smiles.

THE ETIQUETTE OF INFERTILITY

XVII. Navigating Children's Birthday Parties

It is natural to hate everyone and everything, especially on these hormone supplements. There will be hats. Lots of silly hats. Pointed paper hats with flimsy elastic strings that tug unflatteringly against chins. Tempted to snap the string? Don't. It's painful.

Yes, perhaps it is ridiculous to spend $300 on a two-year-old's birthday cake, but this is not for you to judge. "She'll have the pictures," you can say, or assure politely, "It's the most beautiful chocolate Big Bird I've ever seen," and then eat a large hunk from the middle.

When dealing with the other moms, breathe deep. If it helps, imagine a happy place—drift off to early morning fall, the smell of cinnamon and raked leaves, a hot cup of Earl Grey tea. Remember: The Grass is Greener on the Other Side! While you are envying their solid, swift movements, their talent for breaking up temper tantrums and wiping spit, they will walk up behind you and squeeze your waist. They will say, "You are so tiny!" and you should smile and laugh and squeeze your fists.

VIII. Listening to Your Body

Pay attention to every cramp, twist, stomach pain, nausea, food craving, exhaustion. Attune to it like a safecracker, analyzing, listening, hoping for the right combination.

Chart temperatures on a graph more elaborate than the ones you find on GRE tests, measure the elasticity of body fluids, drink products with names like Fertilitea, read your own Tarot cards. Yes, you really are squatting on the bathroom floor with your fingers up there searching for the position of your uterus, and while you're down there remind yourself to call someone about that cracked tile behind the toilet.

Count numbers, learn to add and subtract in your mind like you didn't fail 10th grade algebra. Everything is a cycle—your body, the months, the years, spinning endlessly like the wheel of your bicycle hanging unused for seasons on the garage wall.

Collect coupons for pregnancy tests. Clip them out carefully, staying along the dotted lines, and sort them in with the other Drug Items in your little file folder. Buy enough pee sticks to keep the company in business, but when your husband starts to seem agitated, when he sighs in that way he does when he thinks you've gone on too long about something, begin to squirrel them away in places he would never look. Good examples of this are these: buried inside your yarn basket, shoved in with the tampons, behind the boxes of fiber bars in the pantry.

From Glossary of Terms

P.P. present (Paperwork Parent Present): (circa 1990, Philadelphia, PA) Term coined by your freshman college roommate Jessie, Chinese American, tall, thin, dark-haired girl with a penchant for yoga pants and belly shirts, a girl who'd been adopted by a middle class New Jersey couple that you always thought were nice but smelled like wet dog. The couple lavished expensive presents on Jessie and took her on fabulous vacations. Usage example: "Check out the Tiffany bracelet I got for passing that chem exam. Total P.P present."

Hot Meat Injection: Term first heard coming from the mouth of boyfriend in college as a way to "turn you on" and "suggest amorous activity." Usage example: "Ok baby, are you ready for a Hot Meat Injection?" The same boyfriend who, after you both woke from a night of particularly hard drinking, insisted you take three birth control pills just in case, even though it made you throw up and you still suspect that maybe that one act messed up everything forever.

Schadenfreude *(German):* Pleasure derived from the misfortunes of others, such as feeling secretly relieved when you hear from your mother that your beautiful, rich cousin in Texas who is also trying to conceive may have an ovarian cyst.

People, Situations and Phrases to Avoid

Acquaintance, two kids under the age of five. Stay-at-home mother. Pregnant again, and holds her belly in her hands like it's a crystal ball. Always has some kind of sauce on her blouse. "When are you going to have kids? Join the misery!"

Hairdresser, every eight weeks for color and trim. In between anecdotes about the vacation to Hawaii and his flooded basement gives you "one more year of messing around" before you need to settle down and "start popping them out." "You aren't getting any younger," he chokes, spraying your face with leave-in conditioner.

Concerned friend, uncontrollable gray roots, cold hands, happily married for 800 years. "Just relax! It will happen when you least expect it," which is the same advice she gave you when you were the last one still single.

Online pregnancy forums, where women use terms like "baby dust," "dh (dear husband)," and cute code names for their periods and believe that standing on your head right before ovulation increases your chances.

Your mother, regretting her decision to have an only child, nightly phone calls, purchasing infant outfits in neutral colors when they are on sale: Just In Case. "Have you tried [insert fertility medical treatment here]?"

The motherfucking OB/GYN waiting room with all those bitches rubbing their bulging bodies while reading *Fit Pregnancy.*

Statistics and Factoids

11.8% of women ages 15-44 are infertile.

About 300 million to 500 million sperm come out in one ejaculation. This large number is needed to ensure conception: even under favorable conditions, only about 200 sperm actually reach the egg. (Those troopers!)

98% of women who are addicted to crack will get pregnant the first time they have unprotected sex. This percentage is slightly lower, but still prevalent, for drunk teenage girls, strict

Catholics attempting the Rhythm Method, that woman Connie who used to bring coffee to all the staff meetings and went on maternity leave five months after she had her wedding, and anyone on welfare.

A study conducted at two university hospitals in Denmark concluded that psychological distress may indeed be a risk factor for infertility in some women. Or perhaps infertility is a risk factor for psychological distress? Which came first, the chicken or the egg? Does it matter? At some point the goddamn chicken got knocked up, unless you're like Marjorie Hampton from ninth grade who wanted everyone to believe it was an Immaculate Conception and all those Friday nights behind the McDonalds with Harvey Pilowski was just them talking.

Sperm can last 3 to 5 days inside a woman. Your husband has lived 7 years with you.

III. On Sex

For a healthy relationship, it is important to try to Have Fun. Remember your husband does not want to be reminded of your basal body temperature or progesterone level when he is kissing your stomach. Try varied poses to spice things up and keep it all from becoming a business transaction—scented oils, massages, feathers on sticks that look more like cat toys, dirty talk, role playing.

Be a Good Sport! Don't stare at the ceiling wishing it was already over. Live in the Moment.

He's still got football on Sundays, poker night, his love for Russian literature and that easygoing, carefree laugh that used to coat you. He's still got his active, strong, BILLIONS of healthy sperm that regenerate every goddamn day and that optimistic attitude that you once thought was a virtue.

Do not play the blame game. It's important to be able to separate what is reality and what is caused simply by your thoughts. He is napping because he had a long day at work, not because he can't stand the sight of your face. He ordered plane tickets for Colorado because it's your birthday and not because he's given up on the fact that you might be too far along to fly in September.

Think about another time, when you were young, when you and your husband were on your first date, cycling through back country of a state park when it started pouring rain and you ducked for cover under the awning of a wood shelter for the park rangers. Laughing like little kids. Remember he kissed raindrops off your forehead and he was still new, a mystery, in that time before you knew he puts ketchup in his chicken soup and is afraid of rabbits. You lost yourself in the moment, trembling on the wet ground, ripping open the condom with your teeth. You let him fill you. Overhead the thunder cracked and the rain pelted the awning like a drum beat. Later you would replay it all in your head, the torn condom, the praying, panicking, worrying while you waited for It, willing It to come, and then finally when It did come, that delirious love for life, the shots of tequila, you and he dancing late in a bar, relieved your mistake hadn't cost you anything. But there in that moment that day, while the mud pooled around your back and your future husband hovered above you panting, thrusting, you let it all expand inside you, you let the rain patter all over your face and the cold wind goosebump your arms and you wondered, crazily, delightedly, what the odds were of getting struck by lightning.

THE ETIQUETTE OF ELOPING

Chapter 3: How to Deal with Difficult People
Part I — The Dinner Party
(Three Days after Your Engagement)

It can be intimidating to enter a room full of strangers, especially your future in-laws' friends. Hold a strong drink as you mingle, but keep track of how often you refill. Remember to smile a lot and nod appropriately. The Ring will be the main point of conversation—avoid any traps that may involve the size or cost of it, and pretend you don't know that his mother is disappointed that you didn't go for something more traditional and well, DIAMOND. When they ask you what exactly the stone is, don't go into a long explanation about how much you love turquoise.

If you feel backed in a corner or bullied into making a decision you aren't comfortable with, pretend to choke on a lemon seed or drop a piece of shrimp on the ground and make a show of having to clean it up. Do not feel pressure to decide on a) the designer of the gown, b) the venue, date and time of the reception, c) if you are going to get married in a Catholic church like Sissy, right, because of course that's the way it should be done, or d) if his three sisters will all be bridesmaids.

No, you do not have to try Uncle Rich's stuffed mushrooms, no matter how many times he hints at it.

Try patting a cold, wet paper towel on the back of your neck, your wrists and forehead. If that doesn't work, open the bathroom window and look out into the cold, dark quiet air, listen to the soft chirp of the crickets and contemplate climbing out and escaping into the woods and living with the little chipmunks who don't really care if you are going to have a Head Table or not. Then close the window, go find your fiancé, and whisper things to him that involve straws and camels and backs.

Part II — Email Etiquette

It would be thoughtful to send a thank you note to your fiancé's cousin who bought you a 20-lb. wedding planner book complete with seven sheets of stickers and rose-scented paper. Written, mailed notes are always best, but if you don't have any stationery, a nice thoughtful email is probably ok.

After sending the email, don't be alarmed when your fiancé's sister's name pops up in your inbox, next to a subject line of **Bachelorette Party Ideas!!!!!!** Should you click on any of the embedded links to online party stores selling products such as penis-shaped straws, naughty dice, paper crowns and sashes and horribly cheap-looking t-shirts, immediately run a virus scan on your computer just to be sure. Then click on "Write New Message" and type a quick email to your fiancé that does not mention anything about any of his sisters. Take a deep breath, leave your office and walk down to the bookstore and buy a grande caramel mocha latte and a road map for Las Vegas.

Chapter 5: The Guest List

The typical Bride-To-Be spends many years even before her engagement dreaming about the details of her wedding—everything from what she will wear to whom she will invite. The non-typical Bride-To-Be is still shocked that she is GETTING MARRIED??? and gets hives thinking about having to walk down a small aisle with everyone in creation she knows staring at her.

Think long and hard about your guest list as you wander through the aisles of the grocery store, choosing essential items such as: Cheez-Its, a nail file, an extra pair of pantyhose (in case the ones you packed catch a run in them like pantyhose ALWAYS SEEM TO DO when you really need them not to), a new travel toothbrush and those yummy Swedish Fish. Should you see the latest copy of *Cosmopolitan* with latest airbrushed photo of latest young, hot, everywhere-you-look movie actress on the cover and a sensational exclamation-pointed headline on the side reading: "What is YOUR Dream Wedding? Take the quiz to find out!," buy it on a whim.

Read it aloud to your fiancé as he drives fast. Make sure to wipe the crumbs of Cheez-Its from your fingers before scribbling names on the back of a napkin—all those you would A-list, followed by the back-ups—before shredding the list into thin strips and watching them flutter out of the car window into the desert.

How to Have a Budget Wedding!

Screw the reception.

Screw the flowers.

Screw the little cheap tin boxes filled with mints that have your first names encased in a shiny silver heart and the date of the wedding embossed on the top.

Screw the DJ who can't pronounce your names and plays "Rump Shaker" when your Aunt Gerty gets out on the floor. In fact, while we're at it, screw all those horrible songs that people only dance to when they are wasted at weddings, such as:

- "We Are Family"
- "Electric Slide"
- "The Locomotion"
- "Hot, Hot, Hot"
- Anything by KC and the Sunshine Band

Screw the never-hot-enough chicken satay and stuffed mushroom appetizers and the insane open bar bill estimation.

Calculate the costs associated with the above and make a list of the things you can do with that money instead. Some suggestions:

- FIRST CLASS tickets to Cairo to see the Pyramids and ride on a freaking camel
- A generous down payment on a new Mini Cooper
- Rent
- Seriously, those $500 Kate Spade boots don't seem quite so ridiculous now, do they?
- An Alaskan cruise
- As many all-you-can-eat seafood buffets as you have ever desired.

On Invitations

Hey Beautiful Bride! So your beau is more interested in watching football than browsing all the stationery stores in your city? Here's your chance! Your perfect wedding invitation would be described as:

A. Heavyweight paper of ivory, soft cream or white, printed in a serif type such as Roman in black or dark gray ink.

B. Heavyweight paper of ivory, soft cream or white, embossed with the family coat of arms or crest at the top center of the page in the same color as the typeface.

C. An environmentally sustainable invitation that can be planted in the backyard and will grow a nice bunch of wildflowers if properly watered.

D. Printed at Kinko's on pale pink paper or whatever is on sale, folded up and stamped so as not to waste money on an envelope.

Are you answering E. for none of the above? A none-of-the-above kind of gal doesn't have a NEED for invitations at all. A none-of-the-above kind of gal chokes on her Slurpee as she thinks about the idea of a family crest (considering HER family barely had enough sense to have a working MAILBOX on the front of their house, let alone a coat of arms!) A none-of-the-above kind of gal hates the color pink, sneezes when encountering any kind of flowers, and thinks formal wedding invitations are for the birds (or at least are for people like Stacey, who bring things like kale and bean sprouts for lunch each day, shop at Macy's and believe that nothing in life is good unless you have a china pattern you can live with).

A none-of-the-above kind of gal also has a fiancé who has no interest in football, but instead spends his Sundays writing songs on his guitar and marking up pages of his poetry books, and is at this moment urging his future wife to put down that stupid magazine and lean over the gearshift to nibble on his sweet-smelling ear, thank you very much.

Music for the Ceremony

Prelude: A program of music that begins a half-hour before the wedding. Try scanning through the radio stations once you cross the Nevada border until you come across something by Jim Croce or Cat Stevens. We recommend something with a love theme, though "Time in a Bottle" might put your fiancé to sleep.

Processional: This music signals the beginning of the ceremony. Think loud organs, half in tune, half out, that scared the pants off of you when you were drifting off a bit in the overly air-conditioned church during your cousin's wedding last summer. Instead, as you walk into the small red-carpeted room of the chapel, note the piped-in muted version of "Pachabel's Canon" and fight the urge to sway.

Ceremony: No hymns or sung prayers here. Your officiant, who may have very cold hands with thick rings on at least three different fingers, should take the time to type up your names and print them out if his handwriting is so atrocious. No, he does not dress like Elvis (even if you secretly wanted him to) and no, he is not going to go beyond the 20-minute time period, but really what did you expect?

Recessional: Choose music that will reflect the joy of your new union— Stevie Wonder's "Sir Duke" has a wonderful trumpet introduction that will sound lively and celebratory as you uncork the bottle of Blanton's stashed in the car and pour two shots in plastic Super 8 cups you remembered to take from the hotel bathroom.

What You Will Not Get

An opportunity to pay back all your friends, especially Tiffany, who made you wear the Pepto-Bismol-calf-length-strapless shiny thing with a large bow above your breasts and dyed satin heels that stained your ankles pink for days after.

A Kitchen Aid mixer, five fruit bowls, two vases, three gold picture frames (one of which has "Man and Wife" engraved along the bottom), a gravy ladle, double old fashioned tumblers, weird lingerie from your sister-in-law, an electronic wine chiller or 800 thread-count Egyptian cotton sheets.

The Dress—yes, you say, you can buy a white dress anytime. This is true. But what you will not get with said dress is all that comes with it—the POWER that you see whenever a bride walks into a room. The hush of the crowd, the tears from the aunties, that wonderful rustling swishing sound that comes when she turns quickly. There will be times in your life when you feel utterly, truly beautiful, but you will not have that Wedding Day Moment that all those lady friends talk about.

There may come a time months after when you feel a twinge of regret. Get in your car. Drive to your parents' house and find your father in the kitchen, his battery-powered radio propped next to the sink, playing the oldies' radio station like always. Grab his hand, pull the dishrag from it. Turn up the radio then and twirl around with him around the breakfast table to "Bring It On Home to Me" by Sam Cooke, perhaps not the song you would've chosen, but beggars yadda yadda yadda. The clincher is you'll have your father-daughter dance, dammit, and when you look up at him and he's tearing up, let him blame it on the onions he just cut.

THE ETIQUETTE OF HOMICIDE

II. On Introductions

Above all, you must be patient.

It may take some time to get a full answer, so don't be afraid of a little bit of silence. Prompting, such as "go on," or "what are you thinking?" or "I'm going to beat your face into mashed potato pulp" will not help and will likely make them nervous. You should also avoid finishing people's sentences when they pause. Give them time to articulate their thoughts in their own way.

Listen carefully to their answers (but never write them down) and give positive feedback, such as, "You're doing a good job" or "That wasn't that hard now, was it?" Avoid threats if at all possible. Be sure to give sincere feedback between questions; if they don't think you mean what you're saying, it won't help you.

Express a positive impression of interacting with them. When it's time for you to part ways, smile and let them know that you appreciated talking with them. If you seem insincere, they may feel discouraged rather than uplifted. It is important to let them know this is nothing personal—it's just your job.

Appendix C — Recipe for Old Fashioned

- 2 oz bourbon whiskey
- 2 dashes Angostura® bitters
- 1 splash water
- 1 tsp sugar
- 1 maraschino cherry
- 1 orange wedge

Mix sugar, water and Angostura® bitters in a tall shaker. Dump in an old-fashioned glass, or if you are traveling, any glass will do. Drop in a cherry and an orange wedge. Muddle into a paste using a muddler or the back end of a blunt instrument (like a spoon, or the handle of a screwdriver). Pour in bourbon, fill with ice cubes, and stir. Drink in three gulps sitting down, shoes off, toes waving into the carpet threads. Repeat. Repeat.

Part 7 — The Dance

There are no rules of protocol. The Client prefers you to use bullets. The gun is like your dick, The Client says. Hold it close, protect it. It makes you Who You Are, they say. A steady hand, scope, sniping away from a great distance.

Prefer something more intimate? A dance, then, with a partner who prefers to hover at the edge of the room, just in front of the floor-to-ceiling velvet drapes. Find him there, approach quietly from behind as not to startle. Put your arms around his and remember the waltz lessons Mrs. Kessel taught you long ago on that gym floor—one two three, one two three—and in Mr. Duncan's home economics class years after that, slicing through chicken quickly, efficiently—with confidence you'd get right through the bone. Trust the knife, silent like a goodnight kiss. Then pirouette your partner out, one two three, one two three. Thank you. Thank you.

Tip the concierge, but not too much. Too much will make him remember you; too little will make him remember you.

Part 10 – Laundromats

Remove a bloodstain when it is fresh. Rinse the clothing in cold water. Then blot the bloodstain with some diluted Tide you buy for $2 in the vending machine in the back.

Laundromats are not glamorous. You never see James Bond in a Laundromat at 3:45 a.m., where the 24-hour fluorescent lights at the front entrance speak easy money for the enormous spiders and their webs. They know how to maximize their kills. Some of them you swear you can see breathing.

Ignore the bums sleeping in the corner or wandering through with wild eyes. Ignore the thump, thump, thump, thump of someone's bed sheets in the dryer. Ignore the smell of piss mixed with fabric softener. Focus on you, on getting through, on getting back.

If all else fails, try spitting on a bloodstain—especially if it's your own blood. Surprisingly, this may help.

On Dreams

Eating late at night makes for more vivid dreams. Eat as early as possible, and avoid drinking heavily right before bed.

Should you wake from one of the Terrible Ones, stand up immediately in the dark and jump up and down until your ankles start to hurt and the blood in your head feels hot. Remember you are here. Remember there is no God. There is just you and the dark and the carpet, the soft shaggy carpet you spent your first reward on that was worth every fucking penny because it is real and cost more money than your father would've spent on a car back in those days, back in New Jersey where all the houses squat sad and droopy and falling apart and fuck that, all that. Don't think about your parents either, those nights. Splash some cold water on your face and burn a fifty-dollar bill in the sunken marble tub.

When the fire dies out, eat the ashes.

THE ETIQUETTE OF ARSON

Prologue (The Fire You Didn't Start)

Stop. Touch the doorknob. It is hot, so step back.

Use the towel. Under the door. It will keep out the smoke.

Smoke will still come. Breathe once and hold, large and deep. Open the window and look down. Jumping more than three stories will kill you.

Remove the towel. Open the door. Watch the fire as it curls, roaring, a sound so loud it amazes you since you always thought fire was quiet. Close your eyes and remember the circus man you saw on television who walked through a pit of fire with bare feet.

Chapter 17 — Tips and Tricks

Start with something easy, like lighter fluid.[1] Buy cans in the grocery store and imagine that you are just a guy planning to grill up some burgers and hot dogs in the backyard, eat watermelon until your

---

[1] *You may have a particular fondness for the* clink clink *of the metal lighter fluid can as you crush it between your hands, the sound much like the rattling coins inside the soup can you kept under your bed, the bank that allowed you to save up for the plastic cat clock you saw in the window of the pawn shop down the street because you liked the way its tail wagged back and forth every time the clock struck the top of the hour.*

face is dripping with red juice, tell the neighbors vaguely offensive jokes.

Later, you may find it is more of a challenge to siphon gasoline from random cars. Milk jugs work. Don't fill from cars in the same area. Spread it out.

Location, location, location, vital in real estate and in fire starting. Your first step to a good fire should be to survey the land around you so you can choose the Best Spot. Here are a few things to look for:

- Abandoned warehouses or old storage facilities
- Structures with tall grass or trees nearby from which to watch the results of your work
- Broken windows—a sign that the Neighborhood Watch has disbanded
- Anything large and saggy and sad that needs saving

Technique Tip! A ground floor room is best. A little goes a long way, so spread your gasoline in a zigzag fashion from the back of the room to the front exit, paying extra attention to dense objects like bookcases, desks or piles of crates. Don't forget to leave a trail at the end, an umbilical cord connecting you to the Best Spot.

It may be the end this time, but there will always be more beginnings.

Things You Wish You Could Say to Your Mother

"Once on the TV, this man died and went to hell. They tied him to a chair and pulled his fingernails off one by one. I wished it was you."

"It is okay for boys to cry in certain situations."

"I am an adult now. Stop telling me what to wear."

"Sometimes I want to scratch your face off like a lottery ticket, only there would be a bunch of zero zeros underneath. I would still feel like I won."

"Do you want to see what I did last week?"

Appendix III — Items that Are Fascinating to Burn

Paper

Rubber bands

Squirrel tails dipped in gasoline[2]

Plastic spoons

Dolls

Dog houses

Mattresses

The attic of your grandmother's house

The letters your mother writes to you from the nursing home

Prologue (cont.)

When you make it out, be sure to let someone know that you are alive. Look for them, your mother, your stepfather. Cough, cough, throat tight not cry when she slaps you. Hear her say the things she's always said before and singed, ten times worse than breathing in your mother's

---

[2] *The tail lit up brilliantly with just one touch of the match, but the squirrel ran out of sight before anyone could really understand what pattern the burn took or how fast it spread.*

cigarettes,[3] and then she will wipe the mascara on the back of her hand. Say, "Where is Barney?[4] And when she spits and screams again "Where is he?" and starts to beat her fists against your blanket, remember the remote control car he gave you that summer for your 10th birthday, but don't cry.

Instead step away. Look up at the house emblazoned in gold and orange and yellow, at the thick black swirls rising, at the house's soul escaping.

It is the beginning of the beginning.

On People

People are not to be burned. Do not burn your mother when she dies, even if she puts it in her will. Pat her foot and cover it with the blanket and nod, but know you could never do that, not after what happened to Barney, not even when she says she wants her remains sprinkled out in the ocean.

People are not to be trusted. People are flawed. People smoke cigarettes in the house and fall asleep with them in their mouths and drop matches on the carpet. It is not their fault, though. They try to love. They try their best.

---

[3] *On one occasion, after she burned a hole in one of the new couch cushions she bought at Walmart that day, your mother spun a creative metaphor involving maggots and your laziness and need for food, but you don't recall the exact wording of the insult, just the way that the vein on the left side of her forehead appeared as blue as those ice pops that you Uncle Lou let you eat the weekend you stayed with him up in Pittsburgh. On another occasion, remember the sweet smell of her perfume as she pressed your face against her sweater, hugging you fiercely and kissing your head when she came home from the casino with $540 from playing the slots.*

[4] *At the funeral, the priest told you exactly where Barney went: up to heaven with the angels, and your mother murmured, "Praise be to Jesus."*

People do not understand. They do not see what you do, the black curls of the soul, the bits of salvation that appear in the flames. They do not see its beauty.

Chapter 8 — The Burn

Once the fire has caught, retreat far enough to not get hurt, but stay close enough to still feel the heat. Look for the colors. Sometimes you can see red, blue, purple, orange, yellow. Sometimes even green. Look at the spaces in between the colors. The black. The white. These are the holes that need to fill. These are the pieces of soul being released.

The purity exists in the holes and the heat. The heat is not orange. The heat is white. The souls are black. Do not take your eyes away. It is important to be a witness to it all. You owe it that much, to watch. You owe it tears if that's what happens, and often it does. There is no pain in that. If it is quiet enough, you can even hear it sigh.

THE ETIQUETTE OF GOSSIP

Epigraph

"Gossip helps facilitate bonds by showing others we trust them enough to share information."

—American Psychological Association

Chapter 43 — A New Town!

So you've moved to a new town! Congratulations! Take comfort in the fact that thousands of adults do it every year, even if most of them weren't dragged away from their beloved city for their husband's new job that requires him to work 80 hours a week.

Think positively! A fresh start! New school for your daughter! Your savings account will grow along with the number of bedrooms and bathrooms and square feet of granite countertops you now own!

Privacy and work/life balance are key. You can afford to work part-time now and spend the remaining hours of your week doing *fun* things like yoga, joining mom's groups, and writing cries for help on Facebook and immediately deleting them!

Your daughter can learn to drive in a field, attend a horse camp, grow a garden. And you, well, you will begin the Great Quest to find some sane person in this place with whom you can make fun of the nutjob guy at the end of the block who sells ammo out of his garage.

For goodness sakes, remember what your sister said: This is not the *Hunger Games.* No one's going to *die* or anything.

From Glossary of Terms

Please don't tell anyone this, but... (phrase): I know you're going to tell someone else but I'm going to tell you anyway.

She'd kill me if she knew I told you this, but... (hyperbole): I am a terrible friend, but this is just way too good to keep to myself.

I swear I won't say anything. (total lie): I'm absolutely telling at least one other person.

O.M.G. (exclamation, interjection): I can't wait to leave so I can go tell someone this.

Chapter 56: Making Friends

Ugh! Moms' groups, you might think. Not for me! However, moms' groups can be a great way to make friends in your new neighborhood. Find one built around other interests besides parenting. Here are some to try:

> **Book clubs,** except for ones that meet at TGI Fridays on a Friday (the irony!), pick mostly Nicholas Sparks books, and then ask you to donate $50 to someone's charity for children maimed in hunting accidents.

> **The Women's Ministry,** except that you're not really religious and all they seem to do is make espresso and discuss school uniforms.

Girl Scouts. Meet other moms plus get to spend extra time with your daughter, who may or may not be blaring '90s love ballads in her bedroom because she's depressed. Become a troop leader and encourage story sharing. Learn to start a fire.

Some Spoken and Some Inferred Interview Questions for the Part-Time Receptionist Position at Botstanlee Sales and Manufacturing

1. Tell us about the gaps in your employment history. Did you really need to take time off to raise your kid? Just the one? For that many years?

2. Are you planning on getting pregnant again?

3. How is 'writing and editing the middle school parent newsletter' a transferrable skill?

4. Are you ambitious?

5. You have an article due, a press release to send out, a meeting in five minutes and one of your co-workers is IMing you because she just found out your boss might be sleeping with the mail clerk downstairs. How do you prioritize and set deadlines for yourself?

6. Why are your hands shaking?

7. How badly do you want to work here?

Navigating the Neighborhood Barbecue

So your husband has already joined a bowling league. Do not be jealous of the easy way that he stands, clutching a beer near the grill, chuckling with the guys. *Be friendly, open-minded*—bring a pitcher of pink lemonade, but stash the bottle of vodka in your purse because you aren't sure if it's that kind of party.

Note several positive signs about Patty, your neighbor: she is funny, she has a tattoo of a dove on her ankle, she owns a copy of the game Cards Against Humanity.

The world is a varied place, and folks with similar personalities get along better. Sarcastic people, for example, tend to get along very well with other sarcastic people. You can test this theory. Sit next to Patty while everyone's eating and compliment her eyebrow ring. Cut the corn off the cob with a knife instead of biting into it. Then say something slightly naughty, but still within the realms of polite society. Such as, "The Randolph children must've had plenty of sugar today." Does she respond:

a) "Yes, well, boys will be boys! Would you like a brownie? Martha Randolph made them, and she's simply the most amazing cook in the world."

b) "Yes, my children cannot handle any artificially dyed foods so we've completely removed sugar and processed foods from our household."

c) "If they don't break their necks on the monkey bars, I might do it for them."

If c), then stay a while. You two just might get along.

Should your daughter disappear for a minute, scan the crowd. You may find she's in the corner of the backyard, laughing—actually laughing!—with a boy her age. If your new friend Patty leans in and whispers, "Oh, look at that! She's found Teddy Benedict! He's the student council president. Your daughter has a good eye," then smile softly, nod, and bring out the bottle of vodka. Let Patty pour it into the pink lemonade while you stir. Serve into red plastic Solo cups and sip.

Say, "His father's not bad either," and when Patty giggles, you can add, "He reminds me of a guy I used to date in college." Watch her laugh, pour more lemonade, lean in and say, "*Really.*"

Two Truths and One Lie

Everyone here thinks Sears is the classiest store.

If you Google "ethnic restaurants" in town, you get Sal's Pizzeria, China Buffet and Taco Bell.

The high school marching band plays "I'll Follow Jesus" during its half-time show.

Appendix H: Six Degrees of a Small Town

Patty and Nancy get pedicures together each month and talk about everything that's going on in the neighborhood.

One time when Nancy's marriage was on the rocks, she made a pass at Doug Benedict, your daughter's new boyfriend's father, but it never went anywhere.

Nancy, whose marriage is still not perfect and who didn't even bother to introduce herself to you at the barbecue, gets her hair done in town by a woman who is good friends with Marissa, who is the assistant to the VP in your husband's division at work.

Marissa plays bridge each month with Samantha Woodbury, whose daughter Fran used to date the Benedict boy.

Fran's dad Albert Woodbury is one of the guys on your husband's new bowling league.

Fran Woodbury is in four different classes with your daughter, and those same four classes are the ones where your daughter has found gum, grease, or spit on the seat of her desk chair.

Girl Scout Badges You Wish You Could Earn

Password Cracker: For resourcefully guessing your daughter uses the dead dog's name as her Snapchat password.

Peacekeeper: For not punching the troop mother who used the words "her kind" to describe the only black mother in the troop.

Successful Abercrombie Shopper Who Didn't Go Deaf or Call Any of the Outfits Her Daughter Tried On "Trampy": For showing courageous restraint and patience in the only store in the new mall that your daughter won't turn her nose up at.

Special Agent: For stalking the school parking lot to look for Fran and the other bitches that threatened to beat your daughter up if she didn't stop holding hands with Teddy Benedict during study hall.

Appendix P: Types of Gossipers to Avoid
(and One to Cultivate)
1. The Bathroom Whisperer

Giggles during a PTA meeting, and then, "Like mother, like daughter."

2. The Passively Direct

"So I heard you're on the same committee as Doug Benedict. Going to be working extra hours on the bake sale promotions?"

3. The TMI

After the PTA president has had too many gin and tonics: "Holy hell, the best thing about bald guys is the way their head feels between your legs."

4. The Disgruntled and Jealous

"Oh sure, my son could've been the student council president too if I was the highest-paying doctor in town."

5. The Helpful

During a Girl Scout troop meeting: "Not to spread rumors, but you know that Fran girl that used to date your daughter's boyfriend? She's not exactly a saint."

Things to Take Comfort In

You are a Scorpio. Scorpios are loyal, fierce, and naturally suspicious. Scorpios do not need more than one or two close friends to survive. Like your sister says, It's not the Macy's Day parade, for Christ's sakes. You don't need a crowd.

Every time you've read your own Tarot cards, the Sun card has shown up, along with lots of Cups.

Actual crickets at night through the window, and not one single car horn or engine.

Should life come crashing down around your ears, you can always stay with your sister.

Your daughter has expressed interest in karate lessons.

The Indian market you found in a strip mall actually carries loose spices and organic produce. If you go in Saturday just before the woman closes up, she'll give you a piece of fresh-baked warm naan and wax your eyebrows in the back.

After several days of sleeping in the spare bedroom, a long overdue date night dinner and movie with you, and reassurance from a buddy at work that no one takes Marissa's snide comments and stories seriously, your husband appears to believe you.

Part III — On Confrontations

So you're not good at them? No problem! There's no need to go fire and brimstone or be McGruff the Crime Dog. Try being direct, but seem concerned. Say, "Hey Patty, did you happen to say anything to Nancy about me and Doug Benedict?"

If she reacts defensively and the skin around her eyebrow ring turns bright red, you can assure her you don't think it was her fault (even though it was) or malicious (even though it was.) Try, "I'm sure you didn't mean anything by it, but somehow it got back to some people my husband works with and I just don't want anyone thinking anything's going on." Try, "You know how a harmless comment can get blown out of proportion!"

Once it's all sorted out, offer up a bit of information of your own to smooth things over with your new friend. An example, "The things I keep hearing about Teddy Benedict's ex-girlfriend! Please don't repeat this, but from what I hear she got a little too friendly with the tuba player in the marching band."

Try not to smirk when she says, "*Really.*"

That night, when your husband smiles and tells you how chipper you seem, wrap your arms around him and ask how his bowling scores have been.

Other Wisdoms from Your Sister

When life hands you lemons, squeeze! A bit of chatter between friends is always fine, but be careful who you trust. Don't say anything over email that you wouldn't want your grandmother or your boss to read. Always look on the bright side, but never directly at the sun. Send your husband flowers just because.

Invite the neighbors over for dinner. Don't wait for a special occasion to eat off the fine china. Never serve alcohol without food.

Your true friends will like you for who you are. Don't worry about what other people say about you. For goodness sakes, sometimes keep your mouth shut, smile, and pour another glass of wine.

THE ETIQUETTE OF DISCRIMINATION

T.R.E.E. (Treating, R___, Employees Equally)

Create a simple diagram that will help your staff understand the mission of the office. Try something like T.R.E.E., which can stand for Treating, Regardless, Employees Equally. The "R" is tricky, so a brainstorm may turn up something better (Regularly? Religiously? Rigorously?), but we like the tree metaphor because it is easy to draw one.

Make a big tree poster and draw all the branches pointing upward, like they are all succeeding. If you have extra time, you can add the names of your employees to all the branches, or even little photos of them. If you don't have time, ask your secretary to do it and then stand there behind her, watching while she cuts them out all wrong.

When the poster is finished, hang it proudly in the break room above the microwave oven that no one ever cleans and that Rajesh stinks up every week with his damn curry rice.

V.O.I.D. (Voicing Our Inner Demons)

Let's look in the mirror. Let's see how your tie matches your shirt. The small green polka dots accentuate the gray pinstripes. Shave your sideburns. Pluck any excess hair from your nostrils—you have a meeting in the afternoon and it is not something you want to worry about when addressing everyone. Make sure that your Rolex watch is fastened securely. Remember to Think Positively. Remember the anonymous supervisor survey that your staff took three years ago, and the glowing reviews you got on personality.

Use music to lift your spirits in the car on the way to work. Sing along loudly—who cares who is looking? Healthy leaders don't dwell on what others may think of them. They assume that no one ever talks badly about them. At the red light, when you look down again at that polka dot tie and remember that your wife gave it to you for Christmas last year, don't let it ruin your Zen-like state. Don't let thoughts of her, with her new boyfriend, destroy your day. Don't carry the bad feeling into the office with you. Don't let it prevent you from holding the door for the large woman struggling with her lunch bag right behind you, even if you want to let it slam in her fat, ugly face. Don't judge her for the large whipped-cream-topped coffee she grasps in her pudgy hands.

It is just a tie.

K.I.S.S. (Keep It Subtle, Stupid!)

In leadership development workshops, the facilitators may have pounded into your head that you need to treat everyone equally. Disregard that—it's nonsense. Is Rajesh, whose wife just delivered their third child, really going to have the same flexibility and concentration at work as your secretary, who drinks SlimFast for lunch and lives alone in an apartment five minutes from the office?

It's not about managing equally, but about managing individually and subtly. Let the women sneak out at 4:30 p.m. on a Friday so they hit happy hour at the right time. Let Rajesh come in late so he can drop the kids off at day care and school. However Michael, Myyyy Callll, who pronounces every single syllable of every single word he speaks, needs a shorter string—if you don't like the way he consistently jumps in during meetings and interrupts you with his Good Ideas, make sure he's getting some extra projects here and there to keep him busy and quiet.

Remember you are The Boss. Therefore you can take longer lunches, even if you frown upon it when others do. You can snag one of the premium parking spaces reserved for visitors, especially if it's raining. You can call off staff meetings on a whim.

Appendix B Reasons to Use Sick Leave on Time Sheets	
Acceptable Reasons	Unacceptable Reasons
Your dog died.	Your fish died.
You wake up coughing blood.	You wake up coughing.
Doctor's appointment.	Hair appointment.
Your wife left you for another man and you drank too much tequila and fell asleep in the basement with your head half inside the box of old pictures and your cell phone clutched in your hand with a trail of text messages you probably should not have ever sent her.	You are Michael, and you say you are sick.

Appendix C
HR Policy

Last updated June 1, 2011, the Human Resources policy states that it is:

Acceptable to:	Unacceptable to:
Under Affirmative Action, hire the Asian-American man with two years of experience over the white male from New York with five years of experience and a similar love for college football (go Badgers!)	Take Jean off the important peanut butter account after she announced she is pregnant, even though she will be out of the office for most of the planning time.
Request to move your parking space away from the smokers' break spot when your upholstery ends up stinking like an ashtray.	Give anyone extra points on their Annual Review for participating in the office softball league—and totally saving the quarterfinals with that amazing line drive down the third base line.
Compliment your staff on their work.	Say anything about Polacks when Stanley forgets once again to put a filter in the coffee machine when he makes a pot.
Breastfeed babies in the lobby.	Drink three gin and tonics at the Halloween party and ask the intern if she is a naughty kitty who needs to be handcuffed.

Definitions and Facts

Discriminate: to make a difference in treatment or favor on a basis other than individual merit. *<Human Resources encourages us to hire minorities for Affirmative Action, thus discriminating against white males.>*

OR:

Discriminate: to mark or perceive the distinguishing or peculiar features of *<I can't help but discriminate that Michael has a distinguishing twitch in his neck when he gets nervous speaking in front of groups.>*

OR:

Discriminate: a: to make a distinction *<discriminate among the latest marketing software programs>* b: to use Good Judgment, to have discriminating taste, as in being able to pick out a decent bottle of wine, not the grocery store drivel you get as Christmas presents.

Racism: the belief that inherently different traits in human racial groups justify discrimination.

The Facts:

You are not racist for disliking Michael.

You do not dislike Michael because he is black, but because he is smug and because he has been walking into your boss's office often and closing the door.

Your wife cheated on her college boyfriend with you, and so you should've seen this one coming a mile away.

You do not dislike black people. There are many African Americans that seem like decent people—the guy who works at Subway who always tells you jokes, Donovan McNabb, your mother's neighbor with the poodles.

Troy Davis clearly would've won a Heisman had he played for Alabama or Texas and not been on one of the worst teams in the country.

It is difficult to relate to men who cannot discuss sports at all. It just is.

It is not your fault that you grew up in an area where all the black people lived in the worst part of town and dealt drugs. In the Big City, where you work, there is Variety and Multiculturalism, but where you grew up the only decent folks you knew were as white as the snow that coats the parking lot in the dead of February and causes all your employees to call you at 6 a.m. to see if they can work from home.

S.L.E.E.P. (Steadily Leading Everyone Even with Pain)

Like Sean Payton and Drew Brees led the Saints to a Division Title the year after Hurricane Katrina swept in, you too must lead by example even in dark times. The best leaders are those who can swallow their personal conflicts.

Keep your head high. Rumors are poison—make sure that your staff knows this. If you walk in on a whispered conversation, ask the culprits directly what they were talking about. Say, "Ooh, I want to be in on the gossip," and then smile, fold your hands over your belly and wait for them to make up something. Know if you do that often and enough, it will help to stop nasty conversations in the office.

Cut out fifteen minutes early. Breathe deeply, in and out, in the quiet cold of your car before starting the engine. Fold in perfect thirds the documents you got from HR, the guidelines they sent you via inter-office mail that outline your rights to free counseling sessions through your insurance. Go home. Make an appointment. Wait five minutes, then call and cancel it, deciding the therapist's voice was too high, too feminine for a man, and you want someone who will understand you. Call the next male name on the list, his voice deep and old, comforting, reminding you a bit of your dad, and keep the appointment this time.

Just hope his office is in a good section of town. Not to be racist or anything, but sometimes the South Side of town has those pockets of immigrants that just wander the streets, waiting to get in trouble.

THE ETIQUETTE OF VOYEURISM

Chapter 7 — Directions to Anatomy Lessons

Anatomy Lessons sits just a bit off Route 11. Look for the tiny sign at the edge of the parking lot. It's an ugly cinder block building, no windows. At night you can see the neon lights reflecting off the door glass. If you get to Amish Markets, you've gone too far.

Pull in the lot past Mike's turquoise Mazda with the dent on the left fender, which will usually be the only car parked out front. Everyone else pulls in the back. Park on the row away from the dumpster, since sometimes when leaving, men will fling their empty bottles at it and miss. Mike isn't liable for any damage to cars in the parking lot.

Sit at the table two rows back from the stage, the one against the wall under the poster of the diagram of the human heart. They say Mike was in medical school for a while, but they never say why he didn't finish. Use hand sanitizer; the tables are moist, sticky.

The stage is small, with one pole on each side. The show always starts with a broadcast of Frank Sinatra's "My Way," and at the end of the song everyone's supposed to scream *or the highway*. Waitresses in nurse outfits will bring you drinks, heavy with ice, light on booze.

Appendix II: (Un)Official House Rules

- Don't choose favorites, even if you find Chelsea's tendency to wear red more exciting.
- Stay in the chair.
- Do not be offended that they never make eye contact.
- If the ladies say no, they mean no.
- Always pay upfront.
- Never call Mike "Doc," unless you want a sandbag for a nose.
- Never order a vodka tonic.
- Do not videotape or photograph the dancers.
- No licking or kissing, ever.
- Don't show photographs of your wife or kids.
- Tip. Always tip.

Myth #22
Strippers are losers with no other job choices.

False! You will note many of the women at Anatomy Lessons are actually taking classes at the local college. Tamara has a PhD in medieval literature and applies for tenure track positions while her fake eyelashes set backstage. Bonnie and Luscious are in some teaching program. Chelsea's hoping to get her associate's degree in bookkeeping and data entry. On her off nights she sometimes sits at the end of the bar and studies, tucking her Hill State Community College pen behind her right ear and biting her bottom lip in concentration. Not that you really pay attention.

Myth #35
Only pervs go to strip clubs.

False! Just like in the wide, wide world, you've got your CEOs, your bus drivers, your attorneys, your real estate agents. You will note Mercedes, VWs, Dodges, and convertibles, motorcycles, minivans. Men with pressed suits and shiny shoes. Farmers in dirty jeans and flannels. Teenagers with fake IDs and their father's aftershave. The Asian men come in groups, laughing, long black overcoats.

Of course you'll still find the seedy types, and though the bouncer is there to watch out for them, it can never hurt for you to also take note. One type to be wary of: short, bald, thick in the middle, with a tight leather jacket that cracks when he bends his arms. Should he slide one of those arms around Chelsea when she's on her break at the bar, clench your fist under the table and practice your breathing exercises.

Natural Hazards for the Outdoor Spectator

Dogs

Neighborhood watches

Mrs. Delmonico's insomnia

Metal garbage cans

Mosquitos

Poison Ivy

Guidelines, Amended

1. ~~Don't choose favorites, even if you find Chelsea's tendency to wear red more exciting.~~ You can have a favorite. Everyone does. Even parents have a favorite child. The trick is to hide that fact from everyone. To not be like your father, whose eyes flickered in pity and shame across the dinner table, whose very soul screamed silently *why can't you be more like your brother.*

2. ~~Stay in the chair.~~ You can stand outside the dressing rooms for five minutes. There's a timer on your phone. Pace and hold the phone up to your ear like you needed a quieter space to have an important conversation.

3. ~~Do not be offended that~~ They never make eye contact, but you can still protect her.

On Escape – What to Do When They Know What You're Doing

Always have two back-up stories for why you are in a given place. For example, you may be in the parking lot because you're thinking about registering for a night class at the community college. In a park, bring a book and some headphones. Turn the pages every now and then.

Even so, occasionally you may find yourself caught. In these cases, determining your accuser's state of mind will help you determine which action to take:

- Attempt to reason with the accuser
- Apologize profusely
- Deny, pointing to your book
- Run

The rules of the game: Do not ever take photos.

The rules of the game: Always try to find a place that gives you cover but also multiple escape routes. As on nature trails, never leave anything behind that wasn't there when you came.

The rules of the game: If it becomes absolutely necessary, volunteer to walk shelter dogs around the nature trails. Or actually register for a night class at the college. If it happens to occur on the same day and time of Chelsea's bookkeeping class, well then isn't that something? Being as authentic as possible makes for a better experience.

From Syllabus: ENG 101 — Intro to Film Studies
Hill State Community College

This course provides an overview to the study of film. We will explore the concepts of film forms and styles and technical innovations, while hitting on the ways that cinema provides a context into broad social issues, structures and concerns.

Week 3: Ideology in Film

Critics for many years have discussed how making movies and watching movies are voyeuristic in nature. Commonly, we sit in a dark theater or room and watch the activities of people on a screen, peek into their lives as through a window, without them aware that they are being watched. Horror films have a very strong sense of voyeurism—often as viewers we are urged to take the point of view of the monster or villain.

Please come prepared with all readings completed on the day they are listed.

Signs You Know Your Friend Is in a Bad Relationship

None of her friends like him. If her family or friends have reservations about him, if they actually have been seen sticking their tongues out at the back of his head and (not verified to be true, but highly suspected) have hocked a loogie in his scotch and water when he was taking a call by the door, you should encourage your friend to figure out why they might feel so strongly about him.

She lies to protect him. You casually say, "Didn't Mike just take your tips?" and she says, "He just holds on to them for me."

He puts her down, in private or in front of others. "Lay off the peanuts, Chelsea," "Those shoes look like they've been run over by a tanker," "What, didn't you have your coffee yet today?" are not loving phrases spoken by a good man.

You've left enough obvious hints that her boyfriend is a big fat jerk, but it never works. Even if you bring him up casually and mention ten or fifteen or twenty specific times when he's acted like a real asshole, doing everything from grabbing her arm a little too hard to flirting with Melissa, you'll probably find she's got a list of rationalizations to counter all of them. Remember: His negative behavior may be the exact thing that attracts her to him.

He *says* he loves her, but doesn't act like it.

If your otherwise smart, beautiful, sweet friend is ruining her life with a pathetic, testosterone-filled, junkie, aggressive, cruel monster, it's likely that he might fill a dark void in her past. Maybe he's the father who was never at her dance recitals, or the brother who drank himself to death. Perhaps she is scarred by past traumas and has no self-esteem. It is your job to make sure she knows her worth, to remind her of her good qualities and that she deserves more than to be trapped in a dead-end relationship with a man who uses Vicks VapoRub to slick down his hair and chews on the end of toothpicks.

Amended Guidelines, Amended

You're a regular.

1. ~~You can have a favorite. Everyone does. Even parents have a favorite child. The trick is to hide that fact from everyone. To not be like your father, whose eyes flickered in pity and shame across the dinner table, whose very soul screamed silently why can't you be more like your brother.~~

2. ~~You can stand outside the dressing rooms for five minutes. There's a timer on your phone. Pace and hold the phone up to your ear like you needed a quieter space to have an important conversation.~~

3. ~~They never make eye contact, but you can still~~

Protect her.

Myth #7
Climbing trees is a preferred method for the outdoor spectator.

False! There are many reasons why you should not do this. The bark hurts your hands and can chip off if you put weight on it. The trunks are too wide to grasp easily. If you do get up there, you're too vulnerable. Any tree that would provide good camouflage to hide you would also obstruct any view you might have.

Better places might be: cars, hotel rooms (high rises), parking lots. For townhouses such as, say, Chelsea's, sometimes the best practice is to go around the back of the building. You'd be amazed at what you can see late at night sitting on a park bench. Amazed at how many folks leave their blinds open.

Remember that women in abusive relationships often make up excuses for their men. Remember that, although you've been going to the gym lately, your muscles are still weak—you can only do three pull-ups before giving up. Remember that you have a reputation in your day job for being an even-keeled manager, someone who pays attention to the details. Remember that your mother is a well-respected teacher in her community.

Flip a coin. Heads, you go in. Tails, you walk. When it's tails, breathe out slowly and squeeze the lobe of your right ear until your eyes water.

From "Visual Pleasure and Narrative Cinema"

As the spectator identifies with the main male protagonist, he projects his look on to that, of his like… A male movie star's glamourous characteristics are not those of the erotic object of the gaze, but those of the more perfect, more complete, more powerful ideal ego conceived in the original moment of recognition in front of the mirror.

The character in the story can make things happen and control events better than the subject/spectator.

Chapter 12: On Being Alone

Take a hot shower, as hot as you can stand. Each time her image crops up, open your eyes and scald them with the water. She is an adult. She makes her own choices.

Step out of the shower. Pat yourself dry. Wipe off the fog from the mirror. Squeeze your cheeks hard until it hurts. You are the protagonist in this story.

Stare at your reflection. There's only one rule in this game.

The first one who blinks is the loser.

THE ETIQUETTE OF ILLITERACY

Glossary of Terms

The Letter "X": Recognize the cross. Jesus died on the cross, but the kind of cross he died on is like another letter of the alphabet and means something different. The cross, or the "X," is usually found at the bottom of documents where you need to sign your name. It is also often used when signaling that something is no good or not allowed. A picture of a phone with the "X" for example means that you cannot call your cousin in that place to ask her a question. However, "X" is not always bad. When you get a letter from your grandniece, and at the bottom she writes several XXX's and OOOOs, it means hugs and kisses.

XL: "X" combined with the letter that looks like half of a square is the size you look for when buying clothes. Simple is better, they say. Solid colors rarely go out of style. Dark wool pants keep you warm. Heels aggravate the spur in your heel, but don't get rid of the black shiny shoes stashed in the back of your closet. Maybe someday.

STOP: White letters on a red 8-sided circle that reminds you of a pizza cutter. Signals cars to stop driving so you can cross the street.

ENTER/EXIT: Go in, go out. If unsure about this, wait around the outside of the establishment until someone else comes by and follow them.

READ: Four letters in yellow on a blue sheet of paper. Look for the signs when you arrive at the building where your class is. Follow them back to the overheated classroom in the basement. While your first reaction may be to hate your teacher, a young black-haired gal with pointy glasses who is young enough to be your daughter, resist the urge to leave at the break. You may notice the older gentleman. His name is Theo. He may watch you from across the room. Eat your sandwich at the back desk and practice breathing to stay calm. Open your textbook to page 13 and note the sweet-looking dog running to fetch a ball. You always wanted a puppy.

Chapter 7 – Food Shopping

Here is $50. Divide your grocery shopping up into small bits throughout the week. Think of it as a chance to get out and get some fresh air. The first trip should be essentials only—bread and ham for sandwiches, milk, cheese, cabbage, flour, potatoes for pierogies and haluski. If they are on sale (the red sticker indicates a mark-down) buy some bananas and mangos—they are still exotic and delicious even after all these years.

Examine the bills you have left after that trip. The money with two numbers on it is worth more than those with single numbers. Use that to judge your next trip to the store, but be careful not to go over: you do not want to be stuck in a long line trying to determine which of the boxes and cans to give back to the cashier.

Choose items you know—the cereal with the green leprechaun shooting candy off his spoon, the canned soup with the picture of simmering chili on the front, the boxed macaroni and cheese bright blue and orange, the frozen meals that never look as good microwaved as they do on the cover of the box. Push your cart past all the mystery boxes with labels you cannot decipher. Their contents are secret, unforgiving.

If you are feeling adventurous select something, anything, to bring home and try. You may get a cake mix of some kind—use it to make *paczki*. You may get pea soup that looks like baby vomit, or canned peaches, which you are allergic to. Or you may get lucky—dried blueberry granola, creamy peanut butter, chicken noodle soup, applesauce, condensed milk.

Remember that any kind of wine will do, so pick the bottles with the labels that please you most.

The Modern Adventures of Dick and Jane
(Part I)

See Jane's mail arrive. See Jane gather it up in her arms. See Jane bring it into the house. See Jane's name on the envelope.

Where is Dick? Dick used to see Jane's mail and help her. Dick paid the bills. Dick went to work, came home. Jane served Dick his dinner.

One, two, three. *Cztery, pięć, sześć.* Thirteen, fourteen, fifteen. The years went by. Dick got sick. See Dick cough. See Jane cry.

Chapter 12 — Why We Love Houses

Houses are familiar, inviting. They do not need words to express themselves. They do not need explanation. In each house is a living room with cushions and rugs that need to be vacuumed, a kitchen with sinks to scour and cabinets to wipe down, bathrooms with toilets to polish and bathtubs to shine. There is order to the house. The good ones are filled with love and family already, and the bad ones just need time, just need your help to make them better.

A dirty house is a challenge. A clean house is an accomplishment. *Każdy człowiek ma coś do zrobienia na tym świecie.* Every person has a purpose in this world.

The best house cleaners go beyond the surface. Pull forward the bookcase and sweep out the dust that gathers behind it. Lift the ceramic duck and dust underneath. Be sure to straighten the bathmat when you put it back on the tile floor. Do not open drawers or look in the closets (and if you do, never, ever speak of the sex toys you find, or the hidden stashes of potato chips and chocolate, or the hand-written journals and wills and Christmas lists in pretty curly writing you wish you could understand). The best house cleaners are day ghosts—only the clean, soft scent should be the hint that you were ever there to begin with.

Neighborhood Landmarks

Two blocks left and one block right is the bus stop.

If you fall asleep and take the green bus more than four stops, then you will end up in a neighborhood where the houses have many broken appliances and dirty toys on their front lawns, scary-sounding dogs bark behind the windows, and teenage boys hover in groups, staring at you, their fists shoved into oversized sweatshirts.

It is shorter to the coffee shop to cut down the small alley just beyond the green mailbox, but risky if it rained recently because of the muddy potholes.

If you take the red bus three stops, get off, then walk until you see the playground and turn left, your doctor's office is the third building on the right. (Note: Remember when arriving at the appointment to pretend not to see the sign-in sheet at the desk but instead state your name clearly to the receptionist and even so, be prepared that she may forget you and you will have to wait a long time before they call you in. Pee before you go.)

We are not sure where the yellow bus goes, so it is best to avoid it.

Shop for fresh produce at the Asian food mart because none of the labels are in English anyway.

Five stops on the red bus puts you in the neighborhood where you clean, the streets where the houses sit further back and the lawns get mowed by professional companies. If it is a nice day, you can walk a few blocks down to the main highway and the pet store. On Saturdays they bring the dogs in to adopt and they will let you pet them. The wet noses are your favorite.

On Job Fairs

Stand quietly in line. When you get to the front of the line, ask for an application. If the lady hands you a pen, shake your head and smile confidently. Tell her you'll feel more comfortable filling out the application at home, where you have more time. Tell her you've heard wonderful things about her company. Do not tell her the truth—that you hear that cleaning offices pays more than cleaning homes.[5] Do not seem desperate.

---

[5] *Cleaning offices, as you'll find out, is more trouble than it's worth. Many offices have LABELS on things that you are not supposed to touch. They have signs of where you are to go and what you are to clean. The cleaning companies have rules you need to sign and checklists to fill out. The pay may be better but the hours are not. And the buildings, at night, seem so impersonal and scary with their flickering light bulbs and humming, unidentifiable machines.*

Fold the application in half and tuck it into your black purse, which you found hidden under some old Christmas ornaments in the back of the Salvation Army store last year and paid for in change, dumping all of the coins out on the corner and then acting busy, acting distracted, until the cashier sighed and counted out the correct amount for you.

Hold your head high when you walk out of the job fair. Ignore the immigrants in the corner, backs bent, hands cupping cell phones as they try to translate the applications for their friends to fill out. Ignore the husky woman standing next to you, making clucking noises with her teeth and shaking her head at you. "Those people," she may say, touching your arm slightly, "I say if they can't read the language then they should go back where they belong."

The Art of the Public Restroom

Always look for the "W," the letter that catches more water, the letter that can hold liquid, that looks upward, looks hopeful. Upside down, "M," is the one to avoid. Menacing. Men. Maddening.

Of course, like all the stupid rules in the stupid English language, there are exceptions. Lots of exceptions. Especially in fancy restaurants that your cousin Catherine and her fancy, pine-tree-smelling, wool-coated boyfriend take you to when they visit. These places often get clever by using puns, or foreign words (you cannot rely on the longer word meaning the women's room) or animals or other slang words.

Sometimes these places will use pictures to clue you in—silhouettes of movie stars, cartoon characters, the colors pink and blue, but sometimes they will not. If not, decide if you're feeling lucky, if you're willing to take the 50/50 risk, or wait for other customers to walk out.

Or just hold it in.

Should you accidentally open the wrong door, apologize immediately. If possible, blame it on alcohol or the damn medication your doctor just put you on. Look any men directly in the face and nowhere else. Avoid breathing in deeply. Back out quickly. In the correct bathroom, splash cold water on your face until the red blotches disappear. Press your lips tightly together until they turn white. Ask yourself where it is that you Belong.[6]

The Modern Adventures of Dick and Jane
(Part II)

Now it is spring again. Hear the birds chirp.

See Jane go to store. See Theo see Jane, smile. Theo would like to help Jane with her groceries. See Jane say no. See Jane look down, blush. Look, Theo says. Look, look. Theo hands Jane a ripe, bright peach. He points, winking. See Jane run.

Jane and Theo like school. Jane writes, look up, look up. Jane draws cloud. Theo draws a heart. Jane makes an "ex" through it. Jane laughs.

Jane likes flowers. *Czerwona*, Jane says. Red is my favorite color.

See Theo fetch.

---

[6] *Where DO you belong? You were born here! Pale white face, skin wrinkled at the corners of your eyes but surely, surely, not that old yet. Your mother was from Poland, but you know nothing of that place. You never traveled out of the state, let alone across a vast, icy ocean to a country that you only know to be cold and poor, that you imagine to be gray, gray, gray every day, even in the summertime.*

THE ETIQUETTE OF INSOMNIA

Rule #1 — Know When to Give Up

Sigh. Toss back the covers. Sigh.

Leave the room, quietly but not too quietly, secretly hoping you might wake your wife a little just so she knows your suffering. Look at yourself in the greenish nightlight of the bathroom. Note dark circles, red, dry eyes. Raise your index finger and thumb to the side of your head and form a gun. Pretend to shoot yourself and make a "puh-chew" sound for greater effect.

Walk downstairs. Step on one of your son's toys with bare feet, those damn robot cars that you told him five hundred times to put back in his room. Kick it in the corner so it turns on briefly and says, maniacally, "Let's get racin'!" Bite the inside of your lip. Cry a little.

It does not feel right to turn on any lights this godforsaken time of the night, so fumble your way around for the TV remote and turn it on, lowering the volume to a murmur. Flip through all the channels five times, those 235 channels that you pay half your damn salary for and can never find anything good on, and settle on an informercial for some veggie appliance that can cut through a solid brick and then still cut beautiful translucent slices of tomato. Call the 800 number to buy it and find that the company is out of business. Turn off the TV.

Survey the refrigerator. Prime items to look for: the half red velvet cake left over from your mother-in-law's birthday, chicken soup, Bud Light Lime, or, in times of desperation, grapes. Cabinet items can include these: Doritos, Goldfish crackers, chocolate, and those disgusting cheese curl things that your son loves.

Eat. Feel bad. Eat again. Leave the crumbs on the counter and the dirty dishes in the sink.

Chapter 11 — Why Tips and Tricks for Falling Asleep Do Not Work

Counting Sheep

Sheep? Really? Remember on your honeymoon in Ireland when you and your wife came across that herd of sheep just standing there (STANDING there, not jumping peacefully over blue clouds one by one, mind you) in the middle of the road—the only road for miles that would lead you back to your overpriced bed and breakfast? Sheep are not peaceful and they do not move, even when you lay on your horn and curse and bash the palm of your hand against the dashboard. Sheep suck.

Counting Backwards from 300

It's boring. And numbers don't distract you from that water stain on the ceiling above the dresser that you never called anyone about; numbers don't distract you from much at all and in fact remind you of just how terrible you always were at math.

Drinking Warm Milk

Your grandmother used to make you drink a glass of warm milk before you went to bed. The smell of hot milk makes you think of old people. And you hate milk anyway, unless it's infused with a lot of chocolate.

Clearing Your Mind

Don't think about anything. Just relax, let the darkness overtake you. It is dark and calm and quiet, except for the ticking of the clock in the hall outside, which reminds you that the smoke alarm in your son's room needs replacing. And you haven't yet done that, so if by chance a fire started he could be killed. Which reminds you that you need to renew your homeowner's policy, and shit, the mortgage is due again. Have you written the check for that? But you'll take care of that tomorrow. Right now, don't think about anything. Focus on the heaviness of your eyes, on relaxing your neck, your shoulders, your hands. Relax your legs. What pants are you going to wear tomorrow? Did your wife ever pick up the dry cleaning? Because you are all out of dress pants, and tomorrow is NOT casual Friday. Dammit.

How to Masturbate in Bed Next to Your Wife Without Waking Her Up

Wait until she has started to snore in that way she has picked up since she was pregnant.

Slow and steady wins the race. Hold your hand up and out to minimize shaking of the mattress. It is not as comfortable, but it is quieter.

Choose one scenario—a supermodel photo shoot, the pool guy interrupting the rich wife sunbathing nude, that weird giant champagne bath orgy in a movie your brother rented during a hunting trip. Focus on that story and don't let other thoughts ruin your concentration.

Wear socks to bed. Use one of them to catch the mess. Ball up said sock and toss just under the bed. Use the other sock on one foot to remind you to pick up the soiled one in the morning.

Appendix A: Sample Soundtrack for 3 a.m.

The National Anthem

Why: The only song you knew the words to when trying to rock your son back to sleep in the middle of the night.

Talking Heads, "Psycho Killer"

Why: Reminds you of college, circa 1980, you and your roomies blasting the entire album late at night while getting ready to head out for an evening of partying.

Paul Simon, "Train in the Distance"

Why: Everybody loves the sound of a train in the distance. Note the Amtrak that runs just a mile from your house, the soft, soothing sound of the horn as it passes through town. Imagine yourself in another life in one of those sleeper cars, the bottom bunk, tucked inside a warm blanket, lulled to sleep by the constant motion (you were always able to fall asleep in a car, too), heading toward a more exciting destination, a long-distance lover perhaps, anywhere but here.

Miley Cyrus, "Party in the U.S.A."

Why: Catchy, yes? All the teenagers love it—and you won't be able to get it out of your head. Ever. Especially when trying to clear your mind and drift off to dreamland. And the Jay-Z song was on.

All About Sleeping Pills

There are red ones and yellow ones and white ones, capsules and tablets, and even liquid forms if you include NyQuil, which you used to find effective in high school on long car rides with your annoying parents. Do not take anything unless prescribed by a doctor, unless they come highly recommended by your brother, who used to work in a pharmacy in high school and since his back injury last fall seems pretty knowledgeable in general about medicine.

Do not take sleeping pills and attempt to operate heavy machinery, like a fork lift or a tractor or, more likely, your Honda Pilot at 1 a.m. when what you really want is one of those blue Slurpees from 7-Eleven.

Do not take if you are intoxicated or may become intoxicated, if you are pregnant or may become pregnant, if you are not able to get a full eight hours of rest, if you ate beans and rice for dinner, or if you have an important meeting the next morning about that promotion at work.

Side effects may include nausea; headaches; hallucinations; paranoia about that stupid comment about old people and warm milk you made in front of your boss, who just admitted his mother into a nursing home; restless leg syndrome; loss of hair (or is that just an excuse?); an uncontrollable urge to pee right when you finally get settled into a comfortable position with your pillow; drowsiness (ha ha—it actually does say that one right on the box); thirst; hunger; depression.

The most common side effect is laying in the pitch dark staring up at the ceiling and still not being fucking able to fall asleep.

How To Make Up After A Fight

No one wants to fight, but we do anyway. Here are some things that you can do to make up sooner and get back on track:

1. **Don't attack, defend, or explain.** Don't start to give reasons for why you were fighting—because she still hasn't made your son pick up his motherfucking toys from three nights ago, because you haven't slept in two days and your eyes feel like they're being rubbed by sandpaper, be-

cause a blind monkey could do the job better than Marty from market-ing—or you will restart the fight.

2. **If you were wrong, admit it.** Admitting when you are wrong will help to build respect and ease tension. Even if you were right that the child needs to learn how to clean up after himself, you may have been wrong in tossing all the expensive wooden train cars right in the trash. For example, simply saying, "I'm sorry that I am a little tired and under pressure and lose my temper occasionally because I work 60 hours a week in order to pay the mortgage on this starter home about an hour away from the city I have to commute to so that you can stay home and watch our son and walk dogs to earn your pedicure money. I should have been more patient," can go a long way toward reconciling.

3. **Deal positively with continued verbal attacks following an argu-ment.** Your wife may say you are an idiot. Don't fan the flames.

4. **Take responsibility for change after an argument.** Do your part to work on whatever valid criticisms your partner had of you. For example, try not to be an idiot.

5. **Reaffirm your desire for a good relationship after an argument.** Keep it *positive.* "I don't want to be stuck in a bad marriage" is neg-ative and invites more attacks. "I love you, and I want us to take an overnight train trip to New Orleans" is positive.

6. **Be mature, even if your partner isn't.** In every relationship, one partner is more mature than the other. If she says, "Don't be ridic-ulous—no one travels by train anymore," do not point out how stupid that is. Instead, show her brochures of the overnight cars and

use the word "romantic" a lot. Let your maturity help to bring your partner up.

Chapter 8 – Getting Through the Day

Borrow your wife's under-eye concealer to mask the purple under each eye. Dab with powder and examine in all lights.

At work, do not attend any meeting without a grande cup of coffee. Come prepared with pen and paper—doodling will help you concentrate and stay alert. Keep eye contact 80 to 90 percent of the time. Resist yawning—it is contagious and will contribute negatively to the general atmosphere of the meeting.

Carry mints in your pocket to mask the smell of the coffee.

If the exhaustion really catches up with you, take the elevator up to the seventh floor where the private bathroom off the hallway has a good lock and a loud fan. Sit on the toilet and bend forward, cupping your head in your hands and Close Your Eyes. Set your iPhone alarm just in case you drift off.

Epilogue – On Sleep

Creep back into bed. Pull the covers up to your chin. Roll to the side and press up against your wife, who smells like the sea. Remember that moment in Dublin when the sun came through the pub window and lit up her hair as she laughed at one of your dumb jokes. She always laughs at your dumb jokes. Whisper, "On our honeymoon, we should've taken the trains instead of driving, don't you think?" When she murmurs, "Mm hmm" and presses her butt just slightly against you, breathe deep and settle your head further into the pillow.

Everything seems better in the morning, your mother used to say. Imagine your mother waving to you from a platform. Imagine yourself being taken away by a large locomotive, its steam rising hopefully into the air, forming little puffs shaped like sheep. Imagine the caboose, disappearing from view, circling steadily into the mountains far, far away. Sleep. Dream.

THE ETIQUETTE OF DEMENTIA

XV. On Saying No

How do you politely tell your oldest son "no" when he asks you where your property deed is? You do not want to seem rude. Try diverting the conversation to topics such as the dripping faucet in the kitchen or the new priest at Sunday mass whose accent is so thick you can't even understand the Our Father.

If your son, who has always been rather condescending since he graduated from law school, won't drop it, we advise coming equipped with an "anchor phrase" that will help you stand your ground. Consider "That doesn't work for me," "I prefer not to," "My chest really hurts"—and repeat your phrase as needed, knowing you needn't say more.

Chapter 1 – Warning Signs

It usually first appears as forgetfulness.

You may find yourself in the middle of the baking aisle in the grocery store and realize you have no idea why you are there. In which case, it is best to grab the nearest can of cherry pie filling and sack of flour and wheel quickly to the cash register. When the employee stocking the canola oil asks you if you are ok, smile brightly and tell him of course you are and could he please move his cart out of the way so you can pass.

You may say to your only grandchild, "Did I ever tell you about the time I met John Denver at the Atlanta airport?" And she may answer, "Duh, only like seventeen million times, Gramsie," in a tone of voice you would call boorish. Chalk it up to adolescence because kids that age are still testing limits.

A great tip: wear the sweatshirt with the penguins. Three penguins, to remember you have three children. Two boys and a daughter in the middle—a daughter who seems eternally unhappy and who you suspect may be a closet lesbian.

When your memory starts to go, you may feel frustrated, which translates sometimes into anger and resentment at the people around you.

You may say to your grandchild, "Did I ever tell you about the time I met John Denver at the Atlanta airport?" and when she smirks at you and says, "No, never, Gramsie," you might want to slap her teeth out, but resist.

Always nod sweetly and smile. In crowds, wait to see if others laugh before joining in merrily, your lips kicking back against your teeth and blood pumping through your body, reminding you you're still alive.

Worksheet #2 — Last Will and Testament

Use this worksheet as a place to record your thoughts. Note this is NOT an official will and testament. You must have your documents signed, dated and notarized.

LAST WILL AND TESTAMENT OF Mrs. T.L.S.

I.

I, <u>Mrs. T.L.S.</u>, residing at [city, state of testator], on [date] being of sound mind, do hereby declare this instrument to be my last will and testament.

II.

I hereby revoke all previous wills.

III.

I direct that the disposition of my remains be as follows:

<u>Cremation? Don't want my body rotting in the ground</u>

IV.

I give all the rest and residue of my estate to:

<u>My children, to be divided equally (don't fight!)</u>

Excluding these items:

<u>My Bible (with family tree) to my daughter Louisa, may you go to church more often</u>

<u>The balance of my savings account to SPCA</u>

<u>Pierogie recipe to the ladies of the Sacred Heart, who've wanted to get their grubby hands on it for years anyway</u>

<u>My good looks and intelligence (ha!) to ...</u>

XXI. On Reminders

Post-it notes will save your life. On the stove, try: Turn Off Burner. On the bathroom door: Is The Water Running? Next to the bedside water glass: Check The Front Lock. Next to the phone: Hide All Post-it Notes When Company Comes.

Appendix Four – Using Rubber Bands

When you were a child it was customary to keep a rubber band around your wrist to zap yourself whenever you cursed aloud. Use it to your advantage now, zap zap zap when the confusion sets in, zap to remind you of that young boy Gregory you used to have a crush on who said things like "shit piles" and "fuck yeah" that you longed to repeat, to feel on your tongue; zap to recall your first taste of vodka; zap to remember that first Christmas you didn't come home to Mom and Dad but went hitchhiking around southern California, before hitchhiking was bad, dust on your behind, sunglasses perched atop your head, and that large backpack that you and your girlfriends kept your stash of pot in.

Zap to remember the penguin sweatshirt. Three babies, one each year during your late 20s. Two boys and the oldest a girl, your only daughter, a sweet loving woman with the longest eyelashes you've ever seen.

On Nursing Homes

It is a New Vision of Living. State-of-the-Art, Modern Luxuries and Amenities. You should not admit how modern-looking and appealing the large, shiny kitchen counters look. They are Alternative Living Communities, spacious, one-floor apartments with walls so thin you can hear the man in the unit next to yours snoring each night and Jesus,

Mary and Joseph, if you wanted to still be living with your husband you wouldn't have divorced him all those many years ago.

(Only, those penguins of yours will say gently, you didn't divorce their father. Remember now? He died 10 years ago, your Gregory, and maybe you'd thought about divorcing him many times—a Modern Man With Expensive Tastes and a Genuinely Wandering Eye!—but you stayed by his side while the cancer ate him up and spit him out like the little worms you used to find in the apples on your grandmother's orchard.) Zap.

Check in at the desk each morning to see if you have any visitors scheduled. Ask casually, so as not to seem desperate. The receptionist is grouchy, and she may remind you of your youngest, a daughter, who you worry hates you. After several weeks, force yourself to stop walking by there. Stay in your apartment with its official little signs to remind you of everything. No more need for the Post-its, now that the penguins are paying Good Money for this place. Even the oven will shut off automatically after an hour. And you don't really use the oven anymore—who would you cook for?

Become fond of the pizza delivery boy—call him Timothy, after your youngest son—but when he acts uneasy know you've gone too far. Zap zap zap and start thawing your own pizza from the frozen food section of the Safeway.

Notes

† While some folks may experience confusion about basic things such as their children's ages, their home address and current events such as the name of that no-good president of ours, there will be seemingly random memories that stick like mildew on a barn. In this instance, June 3, 1971,

denotes the day you bought the new John Denver album "Poems, Prayers and Promises" at the five and dime store downtown.

Chapter 10 – Forgetting

The right thing to do is Make the Best of It. Attend the Tuesday afternoon bingo games, and when you get bingo before Bernice with the weeping eyes, hold off on calling it out so she might have a chance to get her B5. Chat with the men in the corner of the game room who smell like tobacco and raisins.

Stop asking people what their names are and if you've met, because you have met and you should remember their names. Tell the game room men that lewd joke about the black man and the psychologist, and when they laugh, tell it again. Fold the penguin sweatshirt carefully in the back of your wardrobe, cover it with comfortable pajama pants and the Penn State t-shirt one of the men give you one night after it shrunk in the laundry. Let the penguins slide off into the snow, washed out in whiteness, and onto your wrists slip gold bangle bracelets that clang sweetly against the dining room table.

Acknowledgments

I would like to thank all of the friends and family who have helped make this book what it is, either by reading early drafts of stories and manuscripts or providing their knowledge and expertise along the way. Special thanks to Steve Himmer, Ellen Parker, Matt Bell, Michael Czyzniejewski, and Dave Housley for initially publishing several of these pieces and lending their editorial advice. Thanks also to Brandon Wicks, Katie Rawson, John Copenhaver, Beth Posniak, Laura Ellen Scott, Lorrie Bennett, Marcin Wrona and Maggie Popadiak for their help and guidance. I feel great gratitude to Randall Brown and Matter Press for first believing in this nutty little book, and also to Andrew Gifford for being crazy enough to want to bring it back. Much love always to my parents, Ann and Bernard Laskowski, for everything. A special shout-out to my son Dashiell, who gave me great insight for the "Insomnia" story and continues to amaze me every day. And of course, to my talented and supportive husband Art Taylor—for everything from funny voices to late night feedings to excellent mint juleps. You are my star.

About the Author

Tara Laskowski was the winner of the 2010 Santa Fe Writers Project Literary Awards Series. Her story collection, *Bystanders*, was published in 2016. Other fiction has been published in the Norton anthology *Flash Fiction International*, *Ellery Queen's Mystery Magazine*, *Alfred Hitchcock's Mystery Magazine*, *Mid-American Review*, and numerous other journals, magazines, and anthologies. Since 2010, she has been the editor of *SmokeLong Quarterly*. She lives in Virginia.

www.taralaskowski.com

Also by **Tara Laskowski**

"'Short story' and 'thriller' tend to be incompatible genres, but not in the hands of Tara Laskowski. BYSTANDERS is a bold, riveting mash-up of Hitchcockian suspense and campfire-tale chills."

— Jennifer Egan, author of
A Visit from the Goon Squad and *The Keep*

Available everywhere books are sold and directly from SFWP   www.sfwp.com